Penguin Books

WILD FIG

Michael Leunig's   ....res
were first publish...d in Australia in
1965. He was born in Melbourne
and now lives on a farm in north-
eastern Victoria.

Wild Figments comprises pieces that
have previously appeared in the
Melbourne *Age*, the *Sydney Morning
Herald, Nation Review,* or in various
stage productions.

Also by Michael Leunig

The Penguin Leunig

The Second Leunig

The Bedtime Leunig

A Bag of Roosters

Ramming the Shears

The Travelling Leunig

A Common Prayer

The Prayer Tree

Common Prayer Collection

Introspective

A Common Philosophy

Everyday Devils and Angels

A Bunch of Poesy

You and Me

Short Notes from the Long History of Happiness

Why Dogs Sniff Each Other's Tails

Goatperson

The Curly Pyjama Letters

The Stick

Poems: 1972–2002

Strange Creature

Wild Figments

MICHAEL LEUNIG

PENGUIN BOOKS

Published by the Penguin Group
Penguin Group (Australia)
250 Camberwell Road, Camberwell, Victoria 3124, Australia
(a division of Pearson Australia Group Pty Ltd)
Penguin Group (USA) Inc.
375 Hudson Street, New York, New York 10014, USA
Penguin Group (Canada)
10 Alcorn Avenue, Toronto, Ontario, Canada M4V 3B2
(a division of Pearson Penguin Canada Inc.)
Penguin Books Ltd
80 Strand, London WC2R 0RL, England
Penguin Ireland
25 St Stephen's Green, Dublin 2, Ireland
(a division of Penguin Books Ltd)
Penguin Books India Pvt Ltd
11 Community Centre, Panchsheel Park, New Delhi   110 017, India
Penguin Group (NZ)
Cnr Airborne and Rosedale Roads, Albany, Auckland, New Zealand
(a division of Pearson New Zealand Ltd)
Penguin Books (South Africa) (Pty) Ltd
24 Sturdee Avenue, Rosebank, Johannesburg 2196, South Africa
Penguin Books Ltd, Registered Offices: 80 Strand, London, WC2R 0RL, England

First published by Penguin Group (Australia), a division of Pearson Australia Group Pty Ltd, 2004

10 9 8 7 6 5 4 3 2 1

Text and illustrations copyright © Michael Leunig 2004
The story 'The Garden' was previously published in *Gardenesque*
(Richard Aitken, Miegunyah Press in conjunction with the State Library of Victoria, 2004)
The moral right of the author has been asserted

Design by George Dale © Penguin Group (Australia)
Cover artwork by Michael Leunig
Typeset in Perpetua by Midland Typesetters, Maryborough, Australia
Printed and bound in Australia by McPherson's Printing Group, Maryborough, Victoria

National Library of Australia
Cataloguing-in-Publication data:
Leunig, Michael, 1945– .
Wild figments.
ISBN 0 14 300353 4.
1. Short stories, Australian. I. Title.
A823.3

www.penguin.com.au

Cul-de-sac

You can go to a lot of trouble and conscientious effort to try to accept that humans are individuals with uniqueness and difference. And just when you're making a bit of progress with all that, the humans abandon difference in favour of weirdness. For there can be no doubt that humans are becoming weirder and weirder. Difference has obviously been superseded. It was too clumsy, perhaps, too laborious. Suddenly humans are drifting in great droves into weirdness. It is a popular, global movement. It is the future. It's where the action is.

If you are merely different and you want to remain that way – and you know how to – then you may be in for a very lonely and perplexing time. You may even be in an evolutionary cul-de-sac, like some quaint, innocent little dinosaur. This may feel weird. This may feel *very* weird. But it is not.

THE CHATTERING CLASSES

Chattering is one of life's natural pleasures. All healthy creatures do it with joyous abandon. There are those, however, who have trouble and need to attend chattering classes to receive help and to find relief. In the chattering classes, they learn to unravel their inhibitions, to relax and flow, and to discover the hidden treasure of their ordinary, natural, convivial chatter.

Unfortunately, there are some who are beyond help and they usually drop out of the chattering classes in a frustrated, miserable and embittered condition, whereupon they sometimes attempt to make a virtue of their failure and dysfunction. In such places as newspaper columns they will attack and condemn the chattering classes in a petulant, mean-spirited and unseemly manner. This is wowserism in all its futility, and as such is actually quite entertaining in a perverse way. But chattering is universal good fun. It is a vivacious, persistent and indestructible human impulse. Chattering classes are helpful, enjoyable and hugely successful. Nattering is also lots of fun, but more about that later.

The Housewife's Guide to Sexual Happiness

You will require firm, comfortable shoes with strong laces, and soles which have a good grip. A stout staff or crook is useful. Carry refreshments; for example, bread, sausage, cheese, fruit and ginger ale. Before getting under way, tell somebody the details of your route and how long you expect to be gone. A colourful beanie will prevent heat loss through the head and will be easy to spot should you get into difficulty. A whistle and binoculars are also recommended. It is always more pleasurable to wend your way, rather than heading forcefully towards a particular point. Wending is a great and fine old art and shall be discussed at some later date.

SATURDAY-NIGHT
LOVE STORY

Pathetic human wretch watches telly in bed with home-delivered pizza. Beautiful, sexy dame melts in hero's arms on telly and hypnotised wretch nods off. Wretch lies down on pizza and dreams of super-special woman. She is soft and warm and delicious. She is in bed with him. Tossing and turning on the pizza, the wretch ravishes her glowing flesh – her moist, sumptuous body – until at last they are fused together in ecstasy, the wretch's lips passionately but gently suctioned onto the mystery of a firm, dark, salty olive.

Wretch wakes next morning. Telly still going. American television evangelist warns wretch to mend his ways. Wretch takes note.

Announcement

A very limited period of time is coming when no festival, celebration or major event will be making a claim upon your existence. Perhaps it could be called ordinary time, or peace, or ordinary life. It has no official name. It may not last very long. There will be no fireworks, nor will there be a release of doves or balloons. There will be no special offers of any kind. No information hotline. And no logo, no poster, no slogan.

There will be the dripping of the tap, the ticking of the clock, and the coming and going of plain and ordinary things. Perhaps you will also hear a bird sing, or a spoon move in a bowl, or a person whistling over the back fence, or the sound of secateurs pruning a rose bush. Who knows? There will be no media coverage, no commentary or analysis. It will all pass unremarked upon. Are you ready?

Chapter Five of
My Autobiography

My interest in the human mind began on a warm afternoon in 1952. After lunching at home, I returned to school on the baker's cart to find the playground in a state of high excitement. Robert Barr had split his head on the log swing. They said you could actually see his brain, and I had missed the whole thing. I was shown a small bloodstain on the gravel behind the incinerator. I had missed a wonderful and chilling insight. I had missed Robert Barr's live brain, his actual mind, where all his thinking happened – his very soul which would one day find its way to heaven or hell.

So profound and bitter was my frustration, so thrilling my curiosity, that I dedicated my life there and then to the miserable pursuit of peeping into the human soul and reporting my observations. Fate is wild. Had I not gone home for lunch, had I stayed and glimpsed Robert Barr's brain as he lay whimpering on the gravel, I could have gone on to become a drunk, a woman-iser, and quite possibly the Prime Minister of Australia.

The Businessman's Burqa

Ban the suit! The businessman's burqa! Men trapped and submissive. Men oppressed and hidden. Men as property. Fundamentalist garment. Not in our country! Zero tolerance!

Free men from the business burqa! Garment of misery. No more cultural baggage. Protect our cherished values. Protect our open society. Say no to mediaeval ways. Ban the business burqa!

The Bottle

Because of his problem with the bottle, he knew that he would always be an outsider. His problem was that he regarded bottles as excellent and beautiful things – simple, durable, reliable, economical *and* poetic. A bottle is possibly the most perfect material human achievement ever, he thought, yet so trashed and shattered – so wasted. In a world that scrambled after shoddiness, that applauded shallow frauds, that rewarded dysfunction and tackiness, it disturbed him that the bottle was so used and abused and overlooked; that it was mostly uncelebrated and unloved. It was the contents that got all the attention, yet the bottle could last for ten thousand years!

Sometimes he would sit holding an empty bottle, contemplating its jewel-like qualities and its probable fate, and feel quite shattered (although he was not a broken man).

Modern Business Opportunities: Private Prisons

Start out small – imprison your soul. Punish it. Don't let it free. A private prison for one.

Now move into a bad relationship. Get stuck there. A private prison for two.

Start an unhealthy family. Keep it together. A private prison for four. Now you're expanding!

Become something like a moneylender. Tempt the suckers and snare them. Screw them with nasty contracts. Quite a substantial little private prison!

Now you're about ready for big-time professional incarceration – steel, concrete and human flesh, your first registered private prison. And remember, no pain, no gain. But you will need that essential early grounding, your humble beginning which will inspire and guide you: the private prison for one.

The Great Opening:
Diary of an Eyewitness

Went to the opening of the entertainment complex. An entertainment complex is a neurotic condition suffered by people who get depressed if they don't get lots and lots of entertainment. Couldn't get into the oak room, the mahogany room, or the chipboard room, but got into the masonite room where people were betting on two blowflies crawling up a wall. The wall collapsed, so I lost my money. Should have backed the blowflies.

There was a tabletop dancer who was also a blowfly. It just crawled around in circles in a pool of beer. Lots of jobs in this place for blowflies. I ate a cold sausage roll which was a bit off. Talk about a high roller!

Got thrown into the river by the wowser squad for not smiling. It was my lucky night, because the tide was going out and I clung to an empty beer can and floated downstream. Eventually I was washed ashore at Coode Island toxic waste dump. At last I felt safe and started to relax. This place had integrity, real class! The poisons were honestly labelled. At last, the real dark and dirty side of town. How exciting! Real adrenalin buzz down here.

Those cream-puff nerds in their monkey suits up the river

would pack their daks if they came down here where the big action is. They're the *real* wowsers – can't face it! They don't know what *real* gambling is, what *real* sleaze is, what a *real* fireworks display is. We do all that pretty good down here. Make your hair curl!

A Fable

The princess danced the night away happily with all the handsome and eligible men. At midnight the clock began to strike twelve and all the men fled from the ballroom. In the rush to escape, every one of them dropped a glass slipper on the dancefloor.

The princess gathered all this footwear together and vowed to search for the owners and so find true happiness. She travelled far and wide, trying the slippers on all the men in the realm. The slippers seemed to fit every man quite comfortably, and this confused her deeply. So now what? Where to now?

The Lost Art of Wine Quaffing

A good wine quaffer is rarely seen these days. Quaffing – true quaffing – requires skill and daring. Special quaffing wine is required to produce the essential and distinctive *quaff!* sound as the wind passes from the mouth down into the gullet. The genuine quaffing sound can best be described as being composed of the following elements: air, liquid, bulk and hollowness. A mysterious combination of these four qualities makes the rich, alluring, hypnotic sound of quaffing, and once heard it can never be forgotten.

The wine is taken boldly through slightly parted lips into a mouth poised in a cavernous manner (which produces the necessary sound chamber). The rushing wine slaps against the back of the mouth and folds over into a small wave. It is important that the tongue lie flat and motionless on the floor of the mouth, so as not to impede the natural draining action. The gullet is suddenly opened just as the small wave flops and breaks on the 'rapids' created by the tonsils. Air rushes into the mouth to fill the gap where the wine was. This *whooshing* combines with the echo of the breaking wave and the gargling/flushing sound. A well-rounded, clearly distinguishable *quaff!* is thus produced.

CHILDREN WHO WILL
NOT LEAVE HOME

Children who will not leave home are becoming a big problem. Sometimes they get into the ceiling and build nests, and cannot be flushed out or dislodged. They travel along power lines at night and visit nests of neighbouring children in the roofs of other houses, where they mate and fight and cause a terrible din. A nest of grandchildren in the roof is a particularly nasty situation and is certainly a major headache.

HE WAS A SAILOR

He was a sailor, but the sea was not around him, it was inside him. A vast, deep ocean inside him, and on it his heart was adrift and alone. Powerful currents pulled him this way and that, pulled him off course. There were wild storms when, sick and afraid, he held on for dear life. Calm days when he drifted in peace. Still nights when he steered by the stars and heard angels singing across the water. How long he had sailed! How little he understood the sea! In the dark depths, unknown to him, mysterious black shapes glided and prowled. He was a sailor and the sea was inside him.

The Magician

There was a magician whose act was stolen by his audience; was stolen by the world around him. A world which had learned all the skills of deception, trickery, juggling and effect. A world which spoke increasingly in brilliant jokes and riddles. The magician had to develop a new role. He decided to become an audience – an audience of one. As such, he positioned himself on a street corner unannounced, unadorned, unprepared.

The passing world yelled witticisms. It performed tricks with everything; with clothes, hair, music, relationships, art, real estate, politics, money, words, food, hearts and minds. Modern life had become an act of cunning, except of course the life of the audience of one. The greatest, truest magician of them all.

TRUE HAPPINESS

How may a man measure his own happiness? He must first go to his cupboard and take out all his neckties. Then he must lay them on the ground, end to end. Then he must measure the length of this line of neckties. And that measurement, that distance, is exactly the same as his distance from true happiness.

LIFE ON EARTH

Owls have no New Year's Eve. Neither can their lives be measured in days, for they are fowls of the night. They are never mentioned in New Year's honours lists — owls are *born* with honour. They make no New Year's resolutions — instinctive creatures do not need resolution. They take no hostages, no drugs, no holidays, no showers. Owls ignore art, religion, politics, sport, clothes, media, waterskiing, music, agriculture, history, gold, furniture, world travel, unionism, photo albums, identikit portraits, maps, telephones, charity, scandal, fashion, omens. Owls like trees, moonlight, sex, food, nests, hooting. Vote 1 Owls!

DESTINY

At the age of twelve, he was spoken to by a divine voice as he stood alone in a windswept paddock. 'You will never be the Prime Minister,' said the voice. 'You will not be a member of parliament, not even a town councillor. Nor will you sit on any board or committee, or be a member of any club or society of any description. In fact, you will never fit into the scheme of anything, and you will be out of harmony with your environment and have no charisma. And this of course means that you will end up working in the media as a political commentator. Goodbye and good luck.'

UNOFFICIAL STORY

Into the hidden caves of ordinary life the people withdraw to take shelter — to light their secret homemade candles and to talk amongst themselves about the war. About America, about Afghanistan, the tragedy, the mess, the President's address. They express forbidden thoughts and, furthermore, forbidden sympathies. And doubts and dark suspicions. They listen to the sacred, outrageous voice of intuition.

Outside, images and words rain down upon the land. The official story pounds the surface of their lives. But in the people's secret caves and catacombs — behind their eyes, beneath their homes — creativity and life go on, elaborate, vast and interconnected. The truth cannot be captured, it is too well protected.

Ordinary Australian

There has been a fresh sighting of an ordinary Australian in East Gippsland this week. A tourist claims to have seen the Australian leap across the road in front of his vehicle at about 11.15 on Monday night.

'By the time I'd stopped and got my camera out, it had vanished into the scrub, but I'm certain it was an ordinary Australian,' said the motorist, who did not want to give his name.

A group of forensic anthropologists from Melbourne University are examining the secret location and have made plaster casts of possible footprints.

'If it's out there, we want to find it and tag it with a microchip so we can study it after we release it back into the wild,' said a spokesperson. 'In spite of all the myth, hearsay and rumour, we actually know very little about the ordinary Australian, but we do believe it will turn out to be something which might make your hair curl and be truly, mindbogglingly *extraordinary*.'

Penal Code

Burglary, forgery, bribery, buggery, thuggery, treachery, trickery, rape – for these things he was sent to Australia as a convict on the First Fleet. In the new colony he was regarded as a model prisoner and a good bloke and he earned an early pardon. He worked hard clearing the land. Before long he owned a luxury unit in Noosa. It was white inside and out. So were his clothes and his Mercedes-Benz. So different from the blackness of solitary confinement.

He also owned nearly all the breweries, newspapers, television stations, supermarkets, political parties, and a host of other things. At the end of each day, he laid his head on the pillow and mumbled to himself, 'Burglary, forgery, bribery, buggery, thuggery, treachery, trickery, rape.'

MELBOURNE
BOG MAN

Council workers found his body in a bog on the banks of the Yarra River. Perfectly intact, the body is estimated to have been lying in the preservative mud for forty years. He is dressed in a pair of Stamina trousers, Bonds Y-front underpants, and a Pelaco shirt with an open neck and the sleeves rolled up. He clutches a crayfish wrapped in newspaper in one hand and a Gladstone bag in the other.

Inside the bag is one bottle of stout and three items wrapped in Christmas paper: a doll, a toy aeroplane made of tin, and a small bottle of Evening in Paris perfume. He is smiling serenely.

Scientists have dubbed him Melbourne Christmas-Shopping Bog Man, and are presently conducting tests to reconstruct the events surrounding his death and a picture of Christmas in Melbourne in 1951. More as it comes to hand . . .

THE VALUE OF WEALTH

Once upon a time there was a researcher who made a great
and wonderful scientific discovery. He discovered the principle
of Sanity and Beauty. This valuable discovery, however, eluded
all attempts to turn it into a product. 'What good is Sanity
and Beauty if it doesn't bring prosperity?' cried the funding
committee. 'What good is prosperity if it doesn't bring Sanity
and Beauty?' responded the researcher. This produced a wealth
of shrugging.

The Invention of Laughter: A Scientific Paper

Long ago, in the dim dark days of primal innocence, there was no such thing as laughter on the earth. In response to the phenomena of life, humans made simple noises. They screamed, yelled and howled, but they did not laugh. One historic day, a man was standing by a deep lake when a large, colourful fish rose up towards him from the depths. Startled and amazed, the man closed his eyes and let out a loud scream of delight. In mid-scream he opened his eyes to behold the wonderful fish, but it had disappeared and all he could see instead was his own reflection – an image of himself screaming at something which was no longer present.

This sudden flash of self-consciousness caused such a shock that the scream was momentarily halted. Then, instantaneously regaining its momentum, the scream continued, with short, echoing interruptions to its energy and confidence as it faded. This produced the strange staccato vocal effect which we now call laughter.

Conclusion: laughter is a confused, broken, self-conscious, unconfident and inhibited scream brought on by the arrival of a mysterious, colourful fish from the deep.

Table Tops

A method has recently been discovered of listening to the hidden messages stored in table tops. Table tops actually record and store in their atomic structure all conversations conducted during meals.

Restaurant tables are of enormous significance for the variety and substance of their recordings. A national archive of restaurant tables is being assembled and the huge process of transcription has already begun. Public access to these transcriptions will be made available under the Freedom of Information Act. Scientists are presently conducting experiments with mattresses, and a major breakthrough is expected very soon.

A Kind of Cartooning

For cartooning, basic, primitive tools and materials are desirable. Ancient technology remains unsurpassed in this activity; archaic knowledge and feelings are applied. A steel nib, sharp enough to draw blood on the finger, is recommended. A good black ink can be improved and enriched by the addition of a couple of tears, or a few droplets of dew gathered from roses of the scented variety. A brush made from wood and the hairs of a wild animal, water collected from a nocturnal rain shower – these things are also most desirable.

The surface of the paper is prepared by staring at it. Not too hard or too focused – a long, gentle gaze will suffice to bring the paper to its readiness. The drawing is commenced, and very soon is in a state of mess. Resisting the temptation to make corrections, the cartoonist begins to play in the mess and drifts into an enjoyable state of semi-consciousness. Drawing is layered upon drawing until the mess has deepened sufficiently and a rich juxtaposition of messes has been achieved. All control is lost and the cartoonist is pleasantly lost in the mess.

At this point, aroused by disorientation, the cartoonist departs graciously from the scene so that time can now play its vital part in the process. A mildly soulful activity is then undertaken: a walk, some nourishment, or the contemplation of the natural world.

Slightly more evolved and mature, the cartoonist returns to the mess of the drawing and stares into it with affection. From the mess a new image begins to present itself, and cries out gently for recognition and salvation. Surprised at first, but then delighted, the cartoonist sets about giving definition to the newborn cartoon. The cartoonist 'brings it up', beholds it with joy and gratitude, then lets it go into the world. The work is done.

OVERLOOKING
MY LIFE SO FAR

In my life I had accumulated many things in my head – too many things. Memories, tunes, facts, fears, visions, loves, etc., etc. As many as possible. In a fertile mind, such things will interbreed. Mongrel visions are born; hybrid memories; inbred, idiot love. It gets very confusing!

I decided it was time for a good clean-up, so I emptied all this out of my head and pushed it into a big heap to sort it out. There it was – everything that was me, all in a big jumbled heap. I walked around it. What a mess!

Then suddenly I saw it in silhouette and realised what it was. It was a heap. A simple heap. You don't sort it out, you climb it. You climb it because it is there. Excitedly I clambered to the summit and raised a flag. I was now looking beyond everything that I knew. The view was simply *magnificent*.

The Comb
of Retrospection

To be on the safe side, I took out the fine-tooth comb of retrospection to run it through my life – to comb out all the dark, dirty bits of my history; the silly, messy, naughty mistakes.

After combing furiously for several hours, I had gotten rid of all the nasty little lumps. I had now turned myself into a piece of human confectionery. What a success! I had attained marshmallowdom, the highest, most attractive and perfect state of being, and the epitome of getting it right. I was also stuck to the chair, but more about that later . . .

SOMETHING FOR THE
SIMPLE-MINDED DAYDREAMER

Nero fiddled while Rome burned. This was seen as arrogant, indulgent and stupid. Now, if Nero had been truly smart, he would have organised a fiddling *contest* while Rome burned. A competition! A match! A fiddling duel! Nobody would have noticed or cared if Rome was burning. No way. Not with a match in progress.

Moral: when any sort of contest is in progress, turn away from it. Go to the window and look out carefully at the world.

GOVERNMENT BULLETIN:
MINISTERIAL CODE OF CONDUCT

The private financial affairs of ministers are best conducted in code. The following bodily signals are readily understood by members of the corporate sector and business community, and are just a few examples from the extensive new code:

Scratching the back: simple, obvious, but effective. 'You scratch my back . . .' etc.

Hands cupped and brought together to form a symbolic empty container: this means 'See, I have a brown paper bag which is completely empty.'

Holding two hands clenched in front of the mouth while clearing the throat: this action represents the playing of the alpen horn, which alludes to the existence of a Swiss bank account.

A side-to-side sweeping motion of the foot very close to the ground in front of you: this is the metal-detector sign. It means 'Believe it or not, although I'm a government minister, my hobby, my relaxation, is fossicking for people's lost valuables every Sunday morning, very early, on Brighton Beach — particularly in front of the navy-blue bathing box. What I might find there with my metal detector in the course of a year is anybody's guess.'

Fall

It was autumn and his heart was full and ripe and ready for plucking. So he went to the art gallery, where all the paintings were turning gold and brown. A sad and wonderful sight. How beautiful they seemed as they fluttered from the walls.

An attendant swept them into piles and set fire to them. The pungent, evocative smell of burning art filled the crisp morning air as he walked out onto the street. A woman drove past with a small pink section of her dress hem flapping from beneath the car door. Tears of gratitude swelled from his eyes. Life indeed was sweet and rich and deep and joyous.

THE TROUBLE
WITH SHOPPING

The shop was too elegant. The changing room was too small, the trousers were too tight. The mirror was too awful, the salesperson poked her head in too soon. He tripped over too easily and rolled out into the shop too clumsily. The cleaner swept him out too unthinkingly. He landed in the industrial waste bin too rapidly, was dumped at the rubbish tip too brutally, where he found a pair of trousers which fitted absolutely perfectly.

A BRIEF HISTORY
OF HUMANS

Humans evolved from the primordial slime. Eventually they established a sophisticated, technological slime, in which they live and work hard for hush money. Sometimes the system breaks down, the power fails, and love pops up, just like that.

THE INSPECTOR
AND THE DONKEY

Once upon a time there was a weapons inspector who set out looking for weapons of mass destruction. Along the way he met an old man wailing because he had lost his donkey.

'Never mind,' said the weapons inspector, 'I'll help you find it.'

'You'll have to carry me,' said the old man. 'I'm lame.'

So the inspector carried the old man on his back as they set off in the hot sun in search of the donkey. They searched in vain for twenty kilometres along the road, until they came to the village where the old man lived.

'A thousand thankyous,' said the old man as he alighted at his doorstep from the back of the exhausted weapons inspector.

The old man's wife opened the door. 'I hope your husband finds his donkey tomorrow,' said the stooped inspector.

'Don't worry,' replied the old woman, 'he usually finds one.' And so the inspector resumed his search for weapons of mass destruction.

The Dance

There once was an inventor whose work it was to invent new dances. His aim was to invent the perfect dance, which is of course an impossibility. At the end of each day, enraged with frustration, he would fling his day's work out onto the street in disgust. The peasants of the town would seize upon these imperfect dances and dance them with great joy and gusto. The inventor worked on in earnest dedication. Alone. The peasants danced their lives away. Together. And so life goes on.

The Origin and Meaning of Tennis

Tennis was invented in Ely, Cambridgeshire in 1632 by Lord Tennis. Lord Tennis suffered from melancholia and felt his sadness to be round in shape and located in his chest. The eccentric lord created a small leather ball to symbolically represent this sadness so that he could contemplate it more effectively. He wondered if his sadness might leave him if he were to throw the ball away, so he threw it over the front fence.

The ball landed in the street in front of a passing minstrel, who took a swipe at it with his lute, and the ball hurtled back to the amazed lord. In great excitement, the lord took his own lute and belted the ball once more into the street, and the first tennis match then took place with the ball of melancholia. The deep symbolism of tennis still lives on to this very day.

FREEDOM OF SPEECH

Yes, I have freedom of speech. Yet I dare not tell the boss he is a pig. I dare not tell Mrs Brown how much her breasts excite me. I dare not tell my friends about that weird thing I did on my holiday. I bite my tongue. I swallow my words. I groan and sigh. Freedom to groan and sigh – yes, that's what I have.

LISTENING

The politicians don't like listening to the people. The people don't like listening to the politicians. The politicians don't like listening to each other, except for gossip. The people don't like listening to each other, except for gossip. Listening can be difficult. Eavesdropping and overhearing – these things are free, exciting and lots of fun, and are more practical and popular than listening.

Notes from the Government Economic Think Tank

The concept of the 24-hour day too restrictive for retailing industry. Twenty-eight or thirty would create greater opportunity. The entire business of *time* in desperate need of deregulation. The calendar and clock too unwieldy and rigid for modern economies.

Law of gravity discussed – needs dismantling or restructuring. Too stifling for efficient commerce. Depresses enterprise. Too cumbersome, slow, heavy. Too evenly distributed.

The matter of *language* was raised. Too regulated and socialistic. Dictionary outdated. Too much fat and dead wood. Could be broken up and privatised. Major opportunities for service providers to offer streamlined, competing alternatives for interpersonal talking.

Human body shape – rationalisation overdue. If a man wants four heads, why shouldn't he have them? Huge opportunities in dental, hairdressing, plastic-surgery industries, etc.

The laws of nature generally too restrictive. Socialist conspiracy suspected. National-security organisation to investigate.

The Life Cycle of the Supermarket Trolley

Supermarket trolleys come ashore under the full moon to lay their eggs in the sand. When the eggs hatch, the young trolleys make their way to the supermarket, where they assemble in the carpark. Now they begin their strange life engulfing and disgorging vast quantities of consumer items.

After several years, when they have reached maturity, the trolleys escape individually into the surrounding streets, and by various routes – drains, canals, rivers – they make their way back to the sea, where they mate in deep water and wait for the full moon to begin the cycle all over again.

SILENCE, PLEASE

Silence, please, a man is listening to his conscience. But what's this? The conscience is talking drivel! There must be some mistake. There must be a crossed line. This is so unclever! Surely this is not a conscience talking – this is a simpleton; this is an oaf, a fool, a hick. Come on, conscience, speak up properly. If you want to be heard, you must understand that you're living in a world of quality time and peak experience, of good design, fine taste, rigorous thinking, general excellence, and constant, reliable epiphany.

Oh my goodness, what's this? Now it's yodelling like a hillbilly. It's yapping like a baboon. It's croaking like a frog. This is barbaric! Now it's hooting like an owl, it's snorting like a creature from some dark, dirty swamp. It's doing wolf whistles. Oh dear, please excuse. This is *so* embarrassing.

How Democracy
Actually Works

After voting, the ballot papers are collected and taken to a furnace. There they are burned to fire a boiler which provides steam for a turbine, which drives a generator and produces electricity. The electricity is then conveyed to the parliament building by a special power line, where it is directed into a forty-watt lightbulb in the gents' lavatory. If you walk behind the building late at night, you can look up and see a dimly lit window and be reassured that your vote *does* matter.

Good Old Heartland

Yes, Heartland, long-suffering, modest, decent, overlooked and down-to-earth. Heartland, where the real people live, the families with old-fashioned values. Heartland, home of the humble folk, the simple folk, the quiet, sensible, moderate people. Not a nasty bone in their bodies, not a bad word to say about anyone. Never complaining. Steady, no-nonsense people just minding their own business and getting on with their lives. Oh, to be like them!

But where *is* Heartland? How do you get there? And, more importantly, how do you get away from there? How do you escape if you get stuck there? And if you do escape, how do you forget the place so that you never again have to feel sick every time a politician uses the word Heartland?

A Candidate's Letter
to the Voters
on Election Day

Dear voters, hallelujah! At last election day is here and I don't have to crawl to you any more and beg for your silly, spiteful, pathetic little votes. No more grovelling, no more putting up with your miserable carping, your moody flouncing, fickle posturing, sanctimonious dribbling; your twee, nasty threats of electoral infidelity; your mean, suburban scrutiny. Hallelujah! Go to hell, crass hoons! Creeps! Jerks! Morons! Get lost! Your day is done. I'll never forgive you for what you have put me through, never. This torment, this blackmail, this hideous indignity and stress. Never, never, never, never! How my sad face aches from false smiling. How my poor hand convulses in pain at the thought of one more senseless, grubby handshake with the people.

The prospect of revenge, however, is my sweetest consolation, and I promise you this: if elected I shall, at every opportunity, pay you all back, vigorously and mercilessly. For what you have done to me, I will get you all and get you good. My loathing and contempt for your ugly, wretched lives will in due course find full and extravagant expression. The system will never work for you. You will be unrepresented. You will have a dysfunctional democracy and all the misery and pain that goes with it. This is my pledge. This is my commitment. How it will please and gratify me deeply to see you all go screaming down the gurgler into oblivion! How I will laugh and chortle and lick my lips!

I am not sending you this letter. I am not even sending it to myself. It's too awful and I don't want to know about it. It shall remain sealed and locked in a dark drawer in my study, and nobody, including myself, shall know of its existence. This is all sounding a bit strange, so I will finish on a bright, positive note. I am a good man. Hatred and anger have no place in my life. I am too busy with civic duty, bonhomie and responsible service to the community.

With best wishes on election day
Yours sincerely
The Candidate

GREAT QUESTIONS OF OUR TIME: WHY DO MEN WEAR SUITS?

Nobody knows the answer to this vexing question. Experts have argued inconclusively for decades, and major research has revealed nothing. The main areas of contention have been: Why are lapels shaped like so? Is the tie a phallic symbol? Is the split in the tail of the coat in any way related to sodomy? What are these buttons on the cuffs for? These creases in the trouser legs – why? Why? What does the word 'cuff' actually mean, and how is it pronounced?

In an amazing breakthrough recently, an observation has been made by a seven-year-old child in France which could be the vital first clue in the process of piecing together this dark mystery. It is as follows: the seemingly useless buttons on the sleeve exactly match the buttonholes on the fly. What are the origin and function of such a weird attachment? When we understand this, we will understand much!

The Psychology
of the Suit

The following courtroom scene could encapsulate the psychology of suit wearing:

'This court has found you guilty of murder, aggravated rape, kidnap, committing an unnatural act, breaking and entering, burglary, assault, cruelty to a horse, smuggling explosives, culpable driving, arson, forgery, attempting to bribe a mortuary attendant, possession of a prohibited animal, and bigamy. But because you have, as a mark of respect, taken the trouble to wear a suit for your appearance before me today, I've decided to let you off with a warning.'

So, do men wear suits in a pathetic, infantile hope of reprieve from some terrible judgement which they feel they deserve? Is it a sheath for the hideous weapon which is the male being? Is it a shame container, or is the suit a garment for deception and fraudulence; a slimy, slippery ruse, cleaned, pressed and symmetrical to conceal a great, inner, unbalanced, filthy shabbiness?

THE DESTINY OF THE SUIT

There is a growing body of evidence to suggest that suits are not garments at all, but are in fact highly evolved lifeforms in their own right, of enormous sophistication and cunning. And that a man does not actually *wear* a suit, but occupies or mobilises it in a subservient function according to the agenda and destiny of the suit.

Why a man should want to do this is not yet understood, but it seems that the victim, or wearer, is beckoned and drawn to enter the suit by mysterious, zombifying powers which are believed to emanate from the lapels. Once encased, the wearer abandons all personal responsibility, identity and integrity. Putting on the tie, with its slipknot, is a symbolic act of spiritual suicide and abdication. The wearing of cufflinks, with their shackling connotations, is a further reinforcement of enslavement, subjugation and 'Don't blame me, I'm just following orders' or 'The suit made me do it.'

Suits actually rule the world and could be invaders from another galaxy. Trouser creases may have an aerodynamic function and the flaps created by the rear split in the coat could serve as steering fins or aerofoils. While the government, the opposition and their respective teams may delude themselves that they constitute opposing forces, they are in fact nothing more than suit mobilisers. Tragic zombies of a higher, crueller, more sinister lifeform which has brought the world to its present state of anguish and is steadily bleeding the planet dry – the suit!

THE REMARKABLE
SUIT STONE OF EL FAZEEL

One of the most significant and amazing discoveries of twentieth-century archaeology was the unearthing of the remarkable Suit Stone at Wadi El Fazeel. The small stone tablet, taken from a burial chamber, is the earliest evidence of the origin of men's suits and is dated 8000 BC. This primitive engraving represents the ancestor of the modern suit, worn by businessmen, politicians and various 'professionals', and reveals that very few alterations have occurred in over ten thousand years.

Text on the back of the stone indicates that the suit was originally a burial garment, the unique and mysterious features of which were designed to help expel the soul from the body, to encourage and assist the soul to depart or flee — a sort of soul poultice. The suit, or death sack as it is more correctly translated, was in effect the container for a soulless body. It is truly difficult to understand how businessmen, politicians and various professionals can favour the suit when one considers its macabre origins.

The Important Question
of Suit Disposal

Although suits will not compost, they can be used for mulching purposes. Consequent rises in soil acidity may be offset with generous applications of lime. Suits do not make successful scarecrows, because birds do not appear to be intimidated by them. A massive industrial operation has been established in Tasmania, based on a new recycling process whereby men's suits are shredded, pulped and fermented on a mass scale, then compressed under extreme high pressure to produce a durable and versatile building material known as suitboard. Large volumes of cheap electricity are required for this process.

A spectacular and attractive Hawaiian-style patio and garden torch can be made by wrapping a suit around the top of a broom handle, soaking it in kerosene and igniting it. Ideal for nocturnal pool parties and barbecues.

LIFEBOAT OF THE WORKING CLASS

Actually, my own personal ship never came in either. And it can't be salvaged because the wreckage is strewn too far and wide. Pieces fell off on the track to Mildura; bits were lost in New Guinea, the Orama Ballroom, the Royal Hotel, Footscray Park – all littered with fragments. It broke up so gradually I never noticed. And I ended up in a barbed-wire canoe, lifeboat of the working class.

How to Prepare the
Christmas Turkey

Approach the turkey calmly and steadily. Speak gently and frankly about your intentions. Sit quietly and listen to the turkey. You might hear something you hadn't considered. Be prepared to alter your plans. Don't push the discussion too hard. Take a break and arrange a further meeting, perhaps in a small café, somewhere cheery and relaxed.

Stroll together – along a beach, through a park, down a cobbled lane. Continue to talk and listen. A strolling conversation is more real, it has a special dignity, it has a poetic outcome. Sit side by side and watch the sun set. Watch the stars come out. Travel together and tell each other of your dreams. Open up your hearts and take comfort in being together.

You will not have Christmas dinner, but so what? You will have peace, divine fellowship, and, most importantly, a feathered friend.

Highlights from the 1995 Tomato Seed Catalogue

Sure Shot: at last, the return of the old-fashioned throwing tomato. These cricket-ball-sized fruits with their mushy flesh and powerful staining properties splatter magnificently on politicians' suits. Just like Grandma used to throw.

Modern Girl: here's a smart, go-ahead little fruit for those who like their tomatoes tough. Pink and pretty on the outside, hard as nails on the inside. Will not soften with age.

Russian Whistler: the famous Russian whistling tomatoes require a quiet corner of the garden to achieve their full, mysterious potential. An eerie presence, and well worth the effort.

Big Beryl: Big Beryl is cuddly, but watch out – she's a back-breaker! Fruits of 300kg are not unusual. These whoppers will scare the pants off your neighbours. Should not be grown on steep hillsides.

SQUIRTY BERTIE: a novelty variety. The fruit has a tough skin which holds the bulging, juicy flesh under pressure. We dare you to bite or cut one of these rascals at a crowded dinner table. Loads of fun, heaps of laughs.

FURBALL BONANZA: a recent development from California. The large, plump fruit is shaped like a pair of buttocks and is covered with a thick grey fur, like a Persian cat. More surprises inside. The jet-black flesh has the texture of a runny brie cheese and smells of shoe polish, but tastes like any good tomato.

THE VISION

There was once a man who became so knowing and sceptical that he could see through everything. While talking to friends, he would look through their heads at paintings on the wall behind them. He even saw through the paintings and the walls they hung on; he knew all about art and architecture. He was so travelled that the horizon too lost its mystery; he knew what was beyond it.

His vision circumnavigated the earth unimpeded until he was looking at the back of his own head, which was so transparent that his vision penetrated it and came out through his eyes again. He was now seeing nothing twice, three times, hundreds of times a minute as his vision looped the earth at the speed of light. This causes the eyes to take on an unfocused, sad and lonely look, which may appear romantic. It is not romantic. It is new romantic.

THE SAD LOSS OF INTELLECTUAL RIGOUR IN DOGS: AN EDITED TRANSCRIPT OF THE 1995 JACK RUSSELL MEMORIAL LECTURE

Ladies and gentlemen, it is indeed a truly lamentable and tragic situation that, except for a few obvious and noble examples, humanity has entirely lost the capacity for intellectual rigour; and the human mind, once the lean, hard, vibrant, erect, well-muscled organ which produced and supported civilisation, has been reduced in recent times to nothing more than an insipid puddle of stale, gooey, sickening porridge, the recipe for which is as follows: one part fashionability, one part depravity, and two parts childish fantasy. Mix ingredients and coddle over a very, very weak flame until the mixture becomes transparent and reeks of sentimentality. *Bon appétit!*

Still worse – and much worse – now domestic dogs appear to be following the same vile and ruinous path and are refusing to face the difficult truths, in what amounts to a disgraceful, wholesale, orgiastic abandonment of disciplined scholarship, intellectual rigour and moral courage. Dog art has degenerated into a squalid, repulsive debacle – an infantile, self-indulgent farce of grotesque proportions. Intelligent discourse, reason, decency and vigorous debate in the canine world have given way to a nauseating proliferation of vain and vulgar fripperies, such as ball-chasing, bone-burying, and mindless barking at sparrows.

The descent of dogs into massive intellectual dishonesty, into flagrant and cynical trivialisations of tough moral questions, into despicable historical revisionism on a breathtaking scale, into extravagant sentimental tail-wagging, and into the unrestrained gratification of the barbaric lust for sausages, all lead me to the sad and grave conclusion that the dog world is sliding towards a hideous catastrophe – the final triumph of mass, unmitigated, rampant, full-blown evil. Thank you and good night.

Our Life in a Bizarre Secret Cult

We are married. We are known as husband and wife. We don't refer to each other as 'my partner'. We are not 'guys'. We don't answer to 'Hey, guys'. Sometimes we answer to 'Hello, folks'. On the odd occasion, we have sardines on toast for breakfast on Saturday morning, with a dash of vinegar, a pinch of salt and a bit of pepper. These are the important little details. We love going to bed early, sometimes with a piece of fruit to eat. A good sleep is one of our greatest pleasures.

We do not talk to computers. We *cannot* talk to computers. We *can* talk to dogs and cats, and we do! Quite a lot, if the truth be known. We have no knowledge whatsoever of *The Simpsons*, which is a lovely feeling and a rare privilege. We consistently avoid sausage sizzles, garage sales, gymnasiums, television sets and cinemas. So there you have it. This is our bizarre secret cult.

OLD RECIPE, NEW RECIPE

So you're one of those single women, thirty to forty years old, who can't find a good man and who think that men are too stupid to appreciate what a ravishingly brilliant creature you are; who think that men are too dull and cowardly to engage your vivacious, intelligent spirit, your proud confidence, your sheer excellence, and the awesome richness of your experience and achievement.

Don't despair. The answer could be quite simple. For instance, has it ever occurred to you that you might be too pompous? Or just too greedy and brattish, or too sanctimonious and hypocritical? Just too up yourself and full of bullshit? Has that occurred to you? After all, it's quite natural to be like that – utterly human.

Or have you considered that you might not presently have the capacity to recognise a good man even if you saw one, and that a good man mightn't want to go near you with a forty-foot pole because you are such a screeching, nasty, scolding tyrant, a pain in the neck, a crashing bore and a sly, ruthless megalomaniac? Just imagine that! After all, it's perfectly normal to be like that, perfectly human, and fairly forgivable too, eventually.

However, if you want a mate, you've got to know how to cook – how to cook up a good relationship. It's no good dreaming one up in the Lounge Room of Excellence, you must prepare for ordinary hard slog; you must roll up your sleeves and cook one up in the Kitchen of Give and Take.

First you must climb into the battered old saucepan of love, where you will marinate in the sauce of sex. Then you shall be covered with the wine of faith, the oil of compassion, and the salt of sin and suffering. Now you are tossed in the pan of chaos and seared by the flame of truth. You are carved by the knife of compromise and served with the spoon of duty onto the plate of acceptance, and garnished with herbs of humility. At this point you may well say grace.

A Herbal Remedy
for Lifeache

You suffer from lifeache. Your whole life is sore; it hurts when you move it. Herbal remedy: take one patch of grass, a mild day, and two large green trees. Lie on the grass beneath one tree and contemplate the other tree. Nap from time to time, or gaze occasionally at the grass. Pain will subside. Lifeache cannot be cured, but you can learn to manage the symptoms.

THE ICONIC

He sat on his chair and thought, I'm sitting on an icon; the chair, in its functional simplicity, is truly a great icon. He sipped his tea and thought, A cup of tea is a great icon also. He looked out the window and thought, What a wonderful icon is the common domestic window. And out there, through the window, the world was full of icons. The world is one big icon, he thought.

And then he thought, I used to be ironic and laconic, but now I'm *iconic*. '@#*!!' he said to himself, and no sooner had the word left his lips than he realised what a great icon it was – this amazing word.

SOLEMNISATION

'We are gathered here today to consolidate this person into a state of complete singleness. If anybody has any problem with that, let's hear about it now or forever remain quiet . . . Do you take yourself to be utterly single, to the exclusion of all others forever?'

'I do. With this ring I single myself, and all my worldly goods are mine and nobody else's.'

'I now pronounce you completely and utterly single.'

The single has the right to kiss herself or himself and to self-sprinkle with confetti. The single has the right to throw the bouquet into the crowd. The single has the right to a reception and a honeymoon. Sometimes honeymoons are a disaster, particularly when singles meet other singles and fall in love, in which case the singleness does not work and must be annulled.

THE INNER TERRORIST

His world had changed since the evil terrorist had entered, so cunningly, into his body while he slept. Now it was living inside him, secretly plotting his downfall and he couldn't locate it or flush it out. Where was it hiding? In his stomach? In his heart? Perhaps the terrorist was lurking in the darkness of his bowels? Maybe it was in his skull, snipping all the little wires and tampering with his brain chemistry, which might cause him to lose control and do something terrible. Heaven forbid!

But worse still, the terrorist could cause his hair to fall out, his flesh to sag and wither, and his entire body to age and weaken – what a vile atrocity! The evil one is everywhere, is *anything*. Death to the evil one, not to us. Heaven forbid!

WHERE IS
THE WET BLANKET?

Somewhere out there the wet blanket relay goes on. Another changeover, another proud carrier, and the wet blanket continues on its journey. Somewhere an original thinker suddenly feels the wet blanket being dragged across his life. The crowds cheer as the wet blanket goes by. 'Power to the wet blanket,' they cry. Some fling themselves in its path so that it will drag over them. 'Change my life,' they cry. 'Soothe my pain.' Across the nation the wet blanket is dragged and dragged and dragged. Every square inch will eventually be covered. Where is it now, that old wet blanket?

The Damsel
and the Knight

Once there was a damsel in distress. She had become a bit of a dragon and it was consuming her. A knight in shining armour confronted the damsel, and seeing her reflection in his shiny breastplate she realised what a dragon she had become, and she didn't like it. In earnest she set about getting this dragon where it belonged and making sense of it.

'You have saved me,' she cried. 'Take off your armour that I may kiss you in gratitude.'

'The removal of armour requires assistance,' responded the knight. So together they removed the heavy armour, and then the damsel embraced him warmly. The knight had never been so deeply touched. He felt immense relief. He felt lighter, less weary, more free.

'That's how I feel too,' cried the damsel joyfully, and after some healthy, passionate kisses, they had some healthy, passionate children. They kept the dragon and the armour, which were useful from time to time, and generally speaking, in their own funny way, they lived quite happily ever after.

Your Sausage Questions Answered

Q: If I buy a sausage, can I ask the butcher to carve 10 per cent off the end of it and keep that bit for himself while I take the major portion and avoid paying the 10 per cent tax which the full sausage would attract?

A: *No. Unless the butcher sends the 10 per cent piece of sausage to the government.*

Q: In that case, could I buy nine sausages and ask the butcher to send an extra sausage to the government?

A: *If you can find a butcher who will do that, then there is no problem. But caution is advised.*

Q: What would the government do with the sausage? For instance, could a modern submarine be built of sausages?

A: *Yes. Defence equipment of high quality can be constructed with sausages. Roads can be surfaced with slices of salami also.*

Q: Can kabana sausage be used as ammunition by
     our boys serving overseas?

A: *Kabana is forbidden as a weapon of war under the terms*
     of the Geneva Convention. The AK47 assault rifle
     is capable of firing 1500 cocktail frankfurts per minute.
     Mortadella sausage can be fired from mortars with
     great accuracy. The name mortadella comes from
     de la mortar.

Yearning Aphorisms

It's not always obvious when a person is yearning. Yearning is an exquisitely private or secret condition. What is yearned is true. To yearn is to see. Yearning is the natural remedy for discontent, agitation, non-specific grievance, prickly sensibility, and similar modern ailments. Yearning is a well-tended hope which has ripened slowly into a sweet, sensuous prayer. Yearning brings poise to the imagination, a pleasant momentum to consciousness, and an angel who plays a lute which drowns out the noise of the traffic. Yearning lifts you up out of the courtroom, away from the judge, the police, the lawyers and the witnesses against you. It raises you out through the window and up into the sunshine and the beautiful blue sky.

Telephone
Sex

Telephone sex is one of the great blessings and benefits of modern life and can be too easily taken for granted. So let us spare a thought for our forebears, who had to do it by semaphore – waving signal flags while perched on rocky, windswept hilltops or barren, icy crags. Or those who had to manage with morse code as they sat hunched at lonely desks, tapping away with one finger at a clicking, mechanical key. Or the carrier-pigeon people – what gifted and dedicated people they were, and such effective and economical writers. Just a few well-chosen words scrawled on a cigarette paper and wrapped around a pigeon's leg. Amazing!

THE FACE

You know you're depressed when you can't quite identify with the face you see in the mirror. You frown, but the face in the mirror seems to be smiling. You poke your tongue out – the face in the mirror purses its lips and looks surprised. You bare your fangs and the face in the mirror grins back at you. It's very strange. You pucker your lips, cross your eyes, puff out your cheeks, and the face leans out of the window and says, 'Are you okay?'

You feel like an idiot. You rush inside to the mirror and see that you also *look* like an idiot. You rush next door and apologise to your neighbour. It's okay, you're not depressed.

Wear and Tear

The strain of being acceptable begins to take its mysterious toll. You can see it in the eyes. All those 'being acceptable' classes, the books, the videos – how to be acceptable – all those rules and exercises. The stress of the constant 'being acceptable' competitions, the grinding performances, the tedium of practice, the cold discipline. And worse still, much worse, the 'being attractive' project: all that desperate running, the exhausting vigilance, the soul-destroying labour.

But wait! Even worse – more hideous and painful – the disgraceful, disgusting activity known as 'acting normal'. Ah yes, that as well. Dear, oh dear, oh dear! The terrible wear and tear, the sheer futility, the tragic waste, the pathetic shame . . .

A GOOD BED

A good bed is like a grand piano, upon which the great sleeps may be performed. Yes, it is from the great sleeps that the most moving and wondrous dreams arise. The great performance is attended by an audience of adoring angels who hover and watch in rapturous silence. Finally the great sleep ends and the sleeper awakes. There is a moment of silence. And then the applause, the vibrant, joyous applause of angels streaming down from heaven. The performer steps down from the grand bed and bows to the audience. The day has begun. A good bed is like a grand piano.

Intellectual Venom

During winter, the poison sacs of intellectuals become swollen with a build-up of fresh venom, making them very prickly and aggressive in early spring. A literary furore or a debate about an art prize can provide an excellent opportunity for the pent-up intelligentsia to release this painful pressure from the brain. Should circumstances fail to provide such an outlet, the intellectual can be artificially milked in order that innocent people of good faith might go about their business in safety.

Many unsuspecting, simple-hearted souls have suffered terrible bites from intellectuals as a result of putting a foot wrong in a dreamy, unguarded moment on a sunny day in spring. If attacked, seize the intellectual firmly and carefully behind the neck and present it with a piece of blank paper stretched over a glass beaker. Savage, rapid, repetitive biting will then occur. When the frenzy subsides, the fangs will retract and the intellectual will become docile, affable and charming. You might be amazed how quickly one of these suave, cute creatures can fill a whole beaker at the slightest provocation or opportunity.

Of course, not all intellectuals are venomous. Some are constrictors. They entwine themselves around their prey and steadily tighten their hold. Comprehensive, methodical squeezing is applied until the heart is cramped and there is no room for the victim to breathe.

Intellectuals have acquired a bad name, but this is largely unwarranted. Left alone, particularly in the mating season, intellectuals are a fascinating and important component of the balance of nature. Their presence too close to the house is cause for concern, however, and before retiring at night, always check under the bed covers.

ANOTHER
LITTLE MYSTERY

He used to talk to himself, but not any more. Now he whispered to himself, and quite frequently too. Wherever he went, the whispering went with him. The trouble was, he couldn't quite hear what he was whispering, it was so soft. Soft, yet it sounded very much in earnest, as if it were an important secret or a dire warning – but he just couldn't quite hear what it was.

One day, he stopped in his tracks. 'Speak up, or shut up and forever hold your peace,' he cried to himself in desperation. After that, the whispering stopped and never returned. He became stricken with a forlorn sense that a huge and vital revelation had been lost to him forever. If only he'd gone somewhere still and quiet and slow and had just listened patiently and been able to hear. If only . . .

MILLENNIUM I

Centuries are inclined to run out of steam just a few weeks before they're officially over. What a pain! What a nuisance! They just sort of grind to a halt like a train which stops a little bit short of the station. And the century just sits there and everyone looks at each other and thinks about how stuffy it is in the carriage and how long this is going to be. It's been such a long journey, staring at those same weary faces. The toilets are quite a mess. People are a worry, they really are, what they get up to. God only knows.

And so the century's just sitting there going nowhere – a few banging and hissing sounds and you're looking out at a very boring, worn-out scene and people have had enough.

Suddenly the word goes round. Everyone has to get out and walk the last bit. The tension is broken. Everybody forgives each other and there's joking and laughing as you all pile out into the world for the final trudge. What fun it's been!

Millennium II

A millennium is a concept which is almost impossible for the human mind to grasp. Perhaps a millennium is most effectively and intelligently understood if it is thought of as a frock or a dress being made by a very slow and patient seamstress. This amazing frock has a few mistakes and some challenging parts, but it is a unique creation which is now nearing completion. And this last important bit is called the hem. The function of the hem is to finish off the millennium and the frock nicely and neatly, and to prevent any untidy fraying or rough ending.

So now we must make the hem on the millennium by ending it neatly today, and folding up the last couple of weeks out of sight, so that today is the fold or crease – the clean, orderly, level and pleasing finish we call the hem. The final weeks ahead must be turned backwards and up, and will eventually be held in place by the hem stitch, which is another brilliant, useful, beautiful metaphor.

Australia Relax
(You're Too Clever by Half)

Australia, relax. You seem rather tense. And embarrassed. This is not like you. It's only the Queen, for heaven's sake. Relax. She's nice! Have you forgotten how to enjoy queens and kings? Their beautiful golden carriages, their great castles and colourful flags? Their guards with swords? These are enjoyable things! Crowns, thrones and ancient jewels, these are sensuous and poetic things. Unless you've gone all prudish. Have you?

Have you gone prudish, Australia? All uptight and fastidious? Is this really you? All correct. Queens are there to be enjoyed. What's the problem with that? Come on, your lips are all tight and pursed. Don't be so mean and grim. Have some! Have some royalty – it's naughty, but it's nice. *Live* a bit. If she waves, wave back. Try bowing, if you please. It's fun.

Oh, Australia, Australia, you're all hyped up. Too much television and abstraction and caffeine. I double-dare you to relax and have some Queen. And yes, yes, of course, have some republic! You'll love it. It's beautiful.

OLD AIR

Very sadly indeed, the peculiar old ways of Australian Rules Football have mostly gone, but one that remains is the continued use of the Old Air in the bladder of the ball used for the Grand Final. The Old Air has been preserved in a special, cast-iron cylinder in a secret vault within the bowels of the MCG for the last sixty-five years. The Old Air is ceremonially drawn from the cylinder each Grand Final eve and carefully pumped into the ball to be used for the big match. At the end of the game the sacred air is returned, with reverence, to the great cylinder, where it remains for another year.

The Old Air was first drawn from the atmosphere of an unknown clubroom in the 1930s, during an after-training pie night/smoke night/social evening, when it was pumped into a Grand Final ball with a bicycle pump. Scientists have recently taken samples of the Old Air for electronic spectrometer testing and have released their findings. The composition of the Old Air is as follows: eucalyptus oil, 9 per cent; camphor oil, 6 per cent; nicotine, 18 per cent; malt and hops, 17 per cent; burnt pastry, 7 per cent; tomato sauce vapour, 8 per cent; hair oil, 10 per cent; human emission gases, 25 per cent.

TALKING DIRTY

They tapped his phone. They heard his conversation. He was having one of those fantasy chats with an anonymous woman, five dollars per minute.

'Patience, simplicity, compassion,' she said to him, 'these are the great treasures. Love your fellow creatures,' she continued. 'Open your heart to nature's beautiful truth. Honour it with courage, wisdom and tenderness, and be of good. Cheer.'

'Yes, yes, yes!' he moaned blissfully as he heard the forbidden words. They heard it all. They recorded everything. And now he was in *big* trouble.

THE JOURNEY

The journey between waking up in the morning and the first cup of tea is precarious and immensely sad. It requires courage. The journey from the first cup of tea to the first encounter with the dog is full of hope and pleasure. The journey from the dog to the desk is difficult, serious and erratic. The journey from the desk to the first daydream is pleasant, winding and mysterious. The journey from the daydream back to the desk is bleak, uncomfortable and dispiriting, yet heroic all the same.

And so the various journeys continue – hundreds of them, until the great circumnavigation reaches its finale – the glorious, triumphant journey from the feet leaving the floor to the head arriving on the pillow.

GREAT UNCELEBRATED
INVENTIONS: THE STICK

The stick was invented in 1272 by Arthur Ernest Augustus Stick, a leech catcher and dealer in Ely, Cambridgeshire, England. Arthur's original prototype was quite small by modern standards and was used for lifting single leeches from the marshes into earthenware containers. News of the Stick of Ely spread quickly, and before long sticks of all sizes and with various functions became common throughout Europe.

To this day, however, nobody has been able to improve much upon Arthur's humble design, the forked stick being probably the only notable development. Folding sticks, double sticks and multi-directional sticks are just a few examples of the many variations which have not stood the test of time. The Stick of Ely is probably the most common, useful, efficient and enduring invention known to humankind, thanks to Arthur Ernest Augustus Stick of Ely, Cambridgeshire, England.

One of the Preambles

We the people of Australia, being of indeterminate origin and inclination, not knowing who we are or what we believe in, and not much caring, yet squabbling and squabbling and squabbling – always bloody squabbling – hurried off our feet, cranky as hell, sick with worry, scared to death, up to our ears in debt, and being fairly illiterate, misled, caged, cooped, processed, drugged, dispirited, feckless, confused, hypnotised, conforming, crass – and pretending that we're *not* any of these things – do hereby declare that it's just one big stuff-up, they're all corrupt, what will be will be, and you're a long time dead. No worries, mate.

ANOTHER TYPE OF PREAMBLE

Here's the deal. We the people of Australia, being an extremely diverse group of fly-attracting, television-watching mammals, do hereby accept the prior occupation of Australia by the Aborigines – except in places like Toorak and Double Bay, where they could never have afforded to live. So there are exceptions based on commonsense.

We also steadfastly accept gender equality, including the right of men to wear women's lingerie. We believe in representative democracy; in fact, anything that represents or even vaguely resembles democracy will do – we're not too fussed about that. And finally, this business about God – we've got no problem with God, provided the Devil gets a guernsey as well. We don't discriminate. So that's the deal. Okay?

Just One More Preamble

We the people of Australia hereby proudly declare that we are one united people bound together by a common destiny and purpose. We also accept that this is quite a shocking and terrible thought, as well as being a blatant, offensive lie.

But, oddly enough, we are a people who are quite able to declare things about ourselves which are not true. We have no problem with that. We do it constantly and call it positive thinking. This is our strength and has made our nation very stupid, dysfunctional and unhappy – but so what? We're the greatest people in the world and we uphold and honour the right of shysters, brutes and fools to shape our society and its future. It's all good for business. We're onto something.

And anyway, we've got the most exciting fireworks display in the world. That alone cancels out all the problems and drugs and all that negative stuff. So there. End of f—ing preamble.

SHOULD GERMAINE GREER BE MENTIONED IN THE PREAMBLE?

For example: We the good folk of Australia do hereby acknowledge the prior occupancy of the country by Germaine Greer. We recognise her pain and anger. We *gleefully* recognise her pain and anger. We recognise it because she reveals it to us so often and in such lurid detail that it's unmistakable. 'She's at it again,' we cry. 'Like a cut snake. What a goer!' We lap it up. We gloat. We chortle. We roll our eyes. We love to see her thrashing about in pain and anger. What a feast! And *what* a marathon!

Prior occupant and national preoccupation – that's her. She does something for us, it's true. So please, no reconciliation in this case, we're all having too much fun.

THOUGHTS ABOUT SAINT VALENTINE'S DAY

Firstly, do not under *any* circumstances attend something like a women's writing workshop on erotic fiction. Secondly, do not wear underpants. Furthermore, drink lots of fluids, and do not skimp or scrimp on balms, exotic oils and emollients. Remember, don't get bogged down with the preamble and beware of carpet burns. And last but not least, the poor, the outcast, the downtrodden, life's cruel injustices – just put them out of your mind and leap on each other. Those things are with us always, but you are with each other but a little time.

THE FESTIVAL OF QUIET
RESIGNATION

Winter approaches. The season of festivals is almost finished. You get to one of the last, The Festival of Quiet Resignation. 'I might as well,' you mumble to yourself.

You arrive. Nobody much has bothered to turn up, but the general feeling of quiet resignation is strong. A plastic bag blows along the ground, yet nobody takes any notice. The main attraction is a mirror leaning against a brick wall. You stand and stare at yourself with quiet resignation. It begins to rain, so you walk about in the rain with quiet resignation. There is a barbecue, but the gas bottle is empty. '*C'est la vie*,' says the man with quiet resignation.

As you leave, you see a member of the organising committee sitting in a broken plastic chair. 'What else would you expect these days?' he murmurs to himself. Fair enough, you think to yourself. And that's it!

The Economy

Once upon a time there was a small child who made
friends with the economy. Every night, when the
guards and keepers had locked up and gone home,
the child would steal into the lonely compound where the
economy was kept. And there in the moonlight the child would
listen carefully as the economy told its sad story — a tale of abuse
and neglect.

'They've stuck things into me and taken things away from
me. They've studied me and blamed me and claimed to know
what's best for me. I'm so sick and tired. I'm out of balance and
angry. I'm *very* angry. That's why I won't co-operate. I don't need
a GST, I need TLC. I need tender loving care. Economies need
love!'

THE GIFT

At this time every year Santa Claus checks his records to see which boys and girls have been well behaved. To see which children have not been too difficult for Mother and Father. To see who has not been too selfish or demanding or disobedient. To see who has been well brought up and is well mannered and pleasant and agreeable and cheerful and helpful and clever and good. To these children he will give a gift which could become extremely useful to them in later life: a big, thick book titled *Understanding Your Depression*.

CRACKING UP

He was eating a hamburger. He was eating a hamburger and listening to the radio. He was eating a hamburger and listening to the radio and talking to a friend. He was eating a hamburger and listening to the radio and talking to a friend and doing a right-hand turn when the car phone rang.

It was his wife. 'I can't stand it any more,' she said, 'this mad, crazy life. I can't cope. Come home and help!'

Hell, he thought as he put down the phone and sped through a red light with the radio blaring, saying with a mouthful of hamburger to his friend and lighting a cigarette, 'It's the little woman, she's cracking up!'

BAREFOOT

Although he never actually sold his soul, he had buried it so deep down within himself that his feet swelled up. So deep down that it was irretrievable, buried under the rubble of the Great Lie which he had gradually swallowed – the Great Lie called the Real World, or the System. He'd swallowed it and it was his own fault. All that was left to remind him of his true spirit was an occasional twitching in his swollen feet where his soul was entombed. As a mark of respect, he went barefoot for ever more. 'It's the real me,' he said, but nobody understood what he meant.

ORDINARY
EVERYDAY CURSES

May your neighbour's house be perpetually renovated by a builder who loves listening to the classic hits of the '70s and '80s. May your wife become infatuated with the ideas of Germaine Greer. May your bottom somehow or other some day make it into *The Guinness Book of Records*. May your favourite café become extremely fashionable. May the indicator lever on your steering-wheel column turn into a pretzel. May you develop an ingrown toenail on a very private part of your body not normally associated with ingrown toenails.

STUFF

There is more *stuff* in the world than ever before. Stuff you can touch. Stuff you can think. Stuff you can use and consume. Stuff you can know with all your senses. The growth of stuff is out of control. It is now being created by means of an unstoppable, exponential chain reaction. Stuff has become a major threat to freedom and happiness. It destroys nature and peace. It steals time and space. It fouls beauty. It is relentless, virulent, invasive and addictive. Stuff makes us exhausted and mad. There is too much stuff!

The following common statements can be taken very seriously: 'I'm stuffed' and 'The world is stuffed'.

THE BANISHED ANGEL

A banished angel, weary and lost in space, found a deserted world and landed on its surface. It seemed quite an ordinary world, but peaceful and beautiful enough; there were flowers and trees, there was gravity and warmth, there was light and shade. The previous inhabitants had outgrown this place. It was not big enough, so they fled to a world of their own making – a world constructed of objects and obsessions, of discourse and distraction, a more *exciting* and *interesting* world.

The angel came upon a footprint, and soon after came face to face with a lone, abandoned soul. They smiled at each other and embraced. The angel and the soul fell in love and decided to make a go of it, their friendship and their neglected world. An angel needs a soul and a soul needs an angel – and they both need a home. They fell in love with their simple planet. At night they lay on their old world in each other's arms and gazed happily at the stars.

One night a great meteor blazed across the sky. It was the exciting new world burning up and disintegrating. 'Make a wish,' said the angel.

'I'm afraid it's too late,' said the soul, 'let's say a prayer instead.'

LIFE AND DEATH

It seems hard to believe, but at last I am dead. I am wrapped in slabs of eucalyptus bark and placed in the branches of some saplings, in the manner of an Aboriginal grave. It is a mallee landscape. Spring has arrived. I am deeply shattered by the injustice of my own death and very depressed about being confined here for eternity in this itchy, uncomfortable bundle. I am hot and my body is starting to putrefy, I suspect.

A dusty track winds past the saplings and a straggling group of people move along it. They are young and fresh-faced. They look relaxed and clean. I hear them laughing and talking. Some of them enquire why I am not going to the party. Somebody holds a mirror up to me and I see that my face is deeply cracked, like the muddy bottom of a dried-up dam. It's quite a shock, and my depression worsens. Even if I were alive, I couldn't go to a party looking like this.

Suddenly I'm standing at the rear of St Patrick's Cathedral in Melbourne. The actor Michael Pate is holding open the door of a crypt and pointing down a grey, cement-brick stairway. He is wearing a black cassock and a clerical collar and is smiling at me. I peer down the stairway and feel a rush of icy, refrigerated air. It hurts the cracks in my face. Everything is grey, rough-cast, cement brickwork. It is modern and feature-less. There are square holes in the walls of the crypt. These are for corpses. Michael Pate is offering me an alternative grave. I am horrified, dumbfounded by this ugly place and by Pate's benign insensitivity. I want to be back in the Mallee.

Then I am back. Wrapped in my bark coffin in the saplings. I have made my choice and here I will stay for ever and ever. It seems dreadfully unfair. I am so miserable. Outside, it is a beautiful day and somewhere there is a party going on.

TRAFFIC

The lights changed to green, but his foot was too slow in getting to the accelerator pedal. The gap between the green light and acceleration was one-fifth of a second. He had delayed the flow of traffic by one-fifth of a second!

Behind him, car horns screamed, sirens wailed, alarms whooped, and the sky turned blood-red. Buildings roared like mad beasts, televisions and radios blasted at him from shops. Exhausts growled and the earth shook as a huge hammer descended from the sky to crush him. He shrank below the window level and his car took off in terror. Like a meteor, he hurtled blindly and wildly to the city rubbish dump, where he was instantly bulldozed under tons of waste.

Entombed beneath the rubbish, he reflected in the reeking blackness upon the shameful and stupid inefficiency of his accelerator-pedal foot, his total unworthiness, his dullness, and the just forfeiture of his place in society.

MORALITY TALE

It begins normally enough – a few corrupt prime ministers and High Court judges. Soon enough, politicians and magistrates are on the take. Then decent people like cops and union officials are feathering their nests. The corruption moves through the food chain, to teachers, bus drivers and grandmothers. ('The winner of the chook raffle is . . . Oh my goodness, it's me, fancy that!') Until what started as a tiny thing ends up at the very core of civilisation – children bribing fairies!

Thank God for fat old Labrador bitches, the only decent members of humanity.

SUMMER:
THE MUNICIPAL POOL,
THE DIVING BOARD,
AND THE MEANING OF LIFE

Your turn has come. You have climbed the ladder. You will fly across the sun. Beneath you waits the pool of life and truth where all souls must struggle to stay afloat. Your flight must last as long as possible. It must be original, powerful, entertaining, inspiring and stylish. You must enter the pool with a mighty splash. You must cause a tidal wave.

You are about to fly, but somebody jumps on the middle of the board behind you. You slip and fall. You catch hold of the board. Somebody stands on your fingers. You lose your grip. You drop. It is a 'pin dive' – there is no splash. The last thing you hear before going under is laughter. At the bottom of the pool you grasp the meaning of life, but weeping is impossible underwater.

Nouveau Mondo

A revolution has arrived. A new class has arisen – the nouveau gloomy. Born under the yoke of cheerfulness, their heritage is a culture of achievement and belief. Diligently, however, they have educated themselves to a condition of anxiety and nihilism. Being ill-bred to such anarchy, they can't quite cope with their acquired despair. They flaunt it with unwitting vulgarity. An interesting paradox, because the nouveau gloomy are obsessed with good taste. Their pursuit of beauty, however, is not nobly inspired, it is driven by a fear of ugliness. The brave new world is marked by the aesthetics of squeamishness.

The true nobility survive quietly in social exile. Born humbly to nothing, they carry it closely to their hearts – faithful and wondrous, at one with a cruel world in disarray.

Can this be so? Is this the end of civilisation? Is the world going stark raving mad? Or am I going it alone?

DROUGHT ADVICE FOR
THE MAN ON THE LAND

So you've had enough of the drought? The farm is blowing away, the garden's dead, and everything looks bloody awful. You want relief? Here's what you do.

First drink one bottle of beer, then grab a long, whippy stick off a dead shrub in the garden. Now go to the fowl yard and corner the rooster. Then whip him. That's right, whip the rooster. Fly into him. Go on, go like stink. Whip him *hard*. HARDER. *HARDER*. Whip him – it's all his bloody fault! Get into him, go on. Whip the mongrel, whip him!

NB: Rooster-whipping is a traditional Australian drought remedy, but is not condoned by Animal Liberation or the RSPCA.

TALKING TO TREES

Talking to trees isn't necessarily madness. Talking rubbish to trees – *that* is madness. Trees can bear a lot, but they don't have wooden hearts. They can bear your woes, they can hear of your happiness, but your clever lies, your cunning defences, your smooth talk – all that learned, stimulating, fraudulent stuff; that tricky, closed-up pseudo-friendliness and charm, so easy and habitual – trees would rather listen to the wind in their branches.

All those automatic, cunning verbal constructions and strategies assembled and enacted between souls to prevent them from simply being together – trees can't hear that sort of thing. It's madness to even try it. Being together requires openness, risk, and the clumsiness of spontaneous words. This bears fruit. The relationship blossoms. Slowly but surely. This is not madness.

THE AWAKENING

You are cruising to a mystery destination. Mid-ocean, night-time. You attend a glittering occasion in the ballroom. You notice a woman who is so rare and beautiful to you that you grow weak, lonely, ecstatic. She dances with the captain and some officers. Dazed with a strange resignation, you move out to the rail and drop limply overboard.

You swim away from the ship to wonder at it all from afar. In the blackness a shark bumps into your leg, and from a mile across the water you hear music, laughter, the clink of glasses. You see the twinkling lights. The ocean floor is a thousand fathoms beneath you. You feel mystical, unafraid.

Then you swim back to the ship and, only just making it, you clamber up a rope, exhausted. The woman is on the deck, alone. She has been searching for you, worrying for you. She helps you over the rail. She warms you in her arms. A tear of relief on her cheek, she kisses you. You nearly faint with joy.

A clock strikes twelve. The ship turns into a live-sheep transport. You are kissing a sheep. You are bound for Libya. Everything smells.

PARABLE

Two thousand feet above Scotland, a tail gunner in a crippled British bomber tears off his burning parachute and clothes and leaps in panic from the airborne inferno. Plummeting naked through the night, he thinks he is about to die. He lands on a deep drift of powdery snow which has settled on some fine spruce branches. This cushions his fall and he drops through it onto a shingle roof, which collapses under him. Finally he lands safely and softly on a thick, warm eiderdown on a large bed beside a beautiful woman in a nightgown.

At that moment the woman's husband enters the room with a cup of steaming cocoa, and in a sudden jealous rage he flings the scalding beverage over the naked airman. The gunner is reunited with his crew in the burns ward of a London hospital.

Moral: God punishes those who survive too extravagantly. You have been warned . . .

Personal Cost-cutting: Reducing Your Outgoings (Think Carefully, Now)

Saying 'Good morning' to five separate people each day is a waste of 3650 words a year. That's 5475 syllables completely down the drain. These are the sorts of personal outgoings which are bleeding you dry and sapping your competitive edge. Or so it seems.

But there's a school of thought which says that saying 'Good morning' to a competitor can lull them into a false sense of security, enabling you to take advantage of the situation and win the upper hand with a relatively low expenditure of energy. In this case, saying 'Good morning' is a winning strategy and a wise investment. Very interesting! So think carefully, now. Are you a numbers person or are you a people person? Hmmm?

SHOULD CHILDREN BELIEVE IN SANTA? SHOULD SANTA BELIEVE IN CHILDREN?

Does childhood really exist, or is it just an old Christmas legend? And if it exists, is it inhabited by actual children? Innocent, hopeful children? Trusting believers? Saviours and renewers? The greatest lovers, the sweetest dreamers?

One person, Santa Claus, still believes in all these things, and each Christmas night he goes out searching for as many such children as he can find. He tiptoes into their homes just for the love of seeing them sleeping. He is so grateful for their existence that he leaves gifts. Occasionally even Santa has his doubts. To him it sometimes all seems too good to be true.

THE HAPPY PRINCE

Once upon a time in the town square there was a meaningful statue called the happy prince. An artist who was flying away from the onset of confusion alighted to rest on the shoulder of the happy price. The statue spoke to the artist: 'There are many bewildered people in this town – strip away my meaning and take it to them.'

So the artist began to strip away the meaningful features and take them to the people. 'You must hurry,' said the happy prince, or you will be caught up in the growing confusion.' But the artist continued fearlessly until all that was left of the happy prince was his naked heart.

The townspeople did not understand hearts very well and were angered and embarrassed by the sight of it. And the artist fell down too exhausted to continue his flight to simplicity. The town council ordered the heart to be removed and replaced with something which could be understood. But nothing could alter the onset of confusion and meaninglessness. Nothing except a sense of mystery, which nurtured the artist and the exiled heart of the happy prince.

DIVORCE

Mum and Dad are divorced. Mum's divorced from reality and Dad's divorced from reality. They've both made new relationships. Mum's got a relationship with the television and Dad's got a relationship with the bottle. Technically, however, I'm not a child from a broken home, but I *am* a child from a broken spirit – some would say well brought up for life in the modern world. There are some marriages that don't break up, they dry up. They evaporate.

SELF-REFLECTION

There was once a man who had never seen himself because he had no mirror. He would stare at the wall where the mirror should have been and wonder about who he was. He would dream and dream about all the possibilities. One day he was given a mirror and his dreams ended. He saw two things. He saw himself. And he saw no possibilities.

THE WRONG SPECIES

Once upon a time there was a man who was not the least bit interested in golf, cricket, tennis, swimming, or games of any description. Nor was he interested in economics or politics or movies, television, newspapers, real estate, restaurants, arts festivals, entertainment or public intellectual debates. It's true! Such a man actually existed, and he was a good man too – an honest, open-hearted man; a warm, cheerful, intelligent soul. Practical, friendly, generous, alert, spirited, reflective and fair-minded.

Without a doubt he was all of these things. And what he was most interested in was freedom, real freedom. Ah yes, it's just that he was born at the wrong time, in the wrong place. And of the wrong species. Yes, the wrong species. Bad luck, dear fellow, bad luck. You'll just have to make a go of it with the way things are. Be careful. Be very, very careful.

Mirror City:
The Final Ridiculous
Solution

To beautify a factory, a clever architect had the building clad with mirrors. It became a reflection of the houses across the road. The house dwellers thought the effect was so clever that they too erected mirror facades. The two sets of mirrors reflected each other, back and forward across the road, at the speed of light. A reflection of a reflection of infinite nothingness. A visual vacuum.

This beautification, this elimination of reality, was such a relief that the entire city was clad and paved with mirrors. It seems ridiculous, but even the citizens took to wearing special mirror clothing. All that seemed to remain were the sounds of the city and a vast sky, which was half covered with marks where the mirrors joined. Life had become a deafening reflection of nothing in particular.

ORPHANS

At an early age they were removed from their emotions. They were taken from their true selves and raised in a harsh, narrow culture of sectarian, political ambition: egotistic, legalistic, cunning, domineering and deceitful. In later life, some of them were reunited with their true culture and traditional ways: the ways of humility, compassion and eternal truth.

But many were not. Instead they won power and formed governments to compensate for the loss within themselves of some central, vital, good thing – some terrible, permanent loss of faith. They are powerful and influential. They are truly the lost generation.

THE COMEDIAN

There was a comedian whose sense of humour became so damaged that he could not earn a living. He claimed worker's compensation and tried to prove to a court how a series of emotional accidents had rendered him unfunny. His evidence described a lifetime of exhilarating joys and sudden, jolting heartbreaks which caused philosophical whiplash. This condition made the business of being funny very difficult, and it was hard to take things seriously too. The confusion was crippling. The court howled with laughter. The case was dismissed.

This Week's Footy Tribunal: The Snake Gets Eleven Weeks

Western Dingos ruckman Wayne McSnakey was suspended for two weeks for racial abuse against Northern Reptiles rover Abdul El Fatwami Kahloohn. On a charge of spiritual and emotional abuse using his index finger against Reptiles forward Bill Smith, McSnakey was rubbed out for a further two matches. On a charge of thirty-two counts of licking Reptiles centreman Bob Spool's neck, McSnakey was found guilty and rubbed out for one week.

Found guilty of the charge of lying on top of Reptiles half-back Alan Smoothie in a degrading and bestial manner for an excessive period of time, McSnakey received a further two-week suspension. As a result of being charged with one count of pinning and fifty-seven counts of pelvic thrusting Reptiles winger Bob 'The Ferret' Burrow, McSnakey was scrubbed for an additional three games. Two counts of pelvic thrusting were not proved.

On a charge of grabbing the umpire's whistle, dropping it into his jockstrap and suggesting in a lewd manner to umpire Brian Bean that he 'come and get it', McSnakey was ordered to undertake counselling.

ON THE MEND

Things were getting too fast, too careless, too dangerous. People were breaking up and breaking down. The footpath was dividing and crumbling. He was afraid. He lost his nerve. He tripped and stumbled. He cried out and fell backwards into his own mouth, down into his deep cry for help. Down and down he fell, swallowed up by his own darkness. Deeper and deeper, darker and darker, until he lost consciousness.

And there he dreamed of a woman who embraced him completely, who bathed him peacefully, who blessed him simply. He awoke in the sunlight and arose from out the back of his trousers. Totally refreshed, utterly secure, perfectly serene. It was definitely a strange situation and there was still much work to be done, but he felt sure that life was on the mend.

The Old, Old Dog

'Buy me! Buy me!' yelled the products, but he couldn't hear them any more. 'Watch me!' cried the television. 'Read me!' cried the magazines, but he couldn't hear them any more. 'Drive me!' screamed the car. 'Notice me!' shrieked the celebrity, but he couldn't hear them any more.

'Hello,' said a gentle voice, and hearing it, he turned to see an old dog. 'Hello, and welcome to a new part of your life,' said the old dog, smiling at him. 'It won't be very flash,' said the old dog, 'and it wouldn't rate very highly in an opinion poll. But there'll be loyalty and warmth and time enough to rest,' said the old, old dog.

Why Dogs Sniff
Each Other's Tails

Once upon a time, when dogs ruled the earth, a gala dog ball was organised and all the dogs in the world were invited. When the dogs arrived at the ball, they checked their tails in at the cloakroom, as was the custom in those happy, far-off days. It was a wonderful, glittering occasion and all the dogs, regardless of breed or background, danced the night away and were thoroughly enjoying themselves.

Until suddenly the fire alarm sounded. The ballroom was alight and an uproarious panic broke out. The vast, yelping pack stampeded to the cloakroom, and in the confusion the tails were mixed up. To this day you will see them sniffing each other's tails as they go about their forlorn search for their own. This is the eternal aftermath of The Night the Dog Ball Caught Fire.

NEAR-DEATH EXPERIENCE

He had heard of near-death experiences and their transforming power, but he had never had one. It seemed to him that much of humanity was near death – the way people watched so much television! The living dead, he thought.

While he was out walking, it occurred to him that modern existence itself might be a constant, near-death experience. A flower truck turned a corner and a load of daffodils spilled from the back and buried him. He lay bewildered for a moment under the glowing yellow heap, and then poked his head out into the sunshine. He saw his reflection in a shop window. He smelled the daffodils. How lovely! he thought. It was a *near-life* experience, and already a transformation was in progress.

SOMETHING OF VALUE

One sunny day, you look down and there it is at your feet – a tiny piece of gold. You pick it up, and as you do you notice the vein in a rock where it came from. Excitedly you begin to dig – you follow the vein downwards. Down, down, away from the sun.

You work earnestly and the years pass. Deeper you follow the lead. Smashing at the rockface, propping the tunnel, exhausting yourself. You begin to fear a cave-in, and by now it is too dark to see the gold. All you can do is feel its weight in your hands. Back on the surface, it's another beautiful day – the same as it ever was.

How to Sleep Well

'Good pyjamas, good sleep' – so goes the old saying. Yet many people do not understand the vital significance of pyjamas in the achievement of deep and restful sleep. Sleeping is a religious activity, a holy communion with the inner world of dreams and darkness. The appropriate ceremonial attire is important for a smooth passage into the land of nod.

Essentially, pyjamas must feel comfortable and look ridiculous. Wearing them is a ritualistic renunciation of the conscious, external world – the world of looking good and feeling stressed. As we approach the cot, pyjama-clad, the ludicrous self is proclaimed, triumphant and free. The vestments of the outer world lie cast off and crumpled on the floor. We look soft and childlike, inept and shambling, primitive and funny. The pyjama fabric droops like tired old elephant skin. The buttons are done up in the wrong holes. The trousers are hitched up nearly to the armpits. The cuffs wag above the ankles. One side of the top is tucked in, the other side hangs out. We have no place in the real world looking like this. We are the stuff that dreams are made of. What freedom! What peace! What blessed relief! Good pyjamas – good sleep.

How to Acquire and Care for Your Little Man

A little man is a wonderful companion and can be purchased from any reputable pet shop. When choosing a little man from a batch, select the most boisterous, the one who pushes the others aside as he rushes to greet you. Lift him from the pen and place him on the shop floor for observation. Look for the following: a nice bright prance, playful aggression, and responsiveness to affection.

Upon getting your little man home, allow him to explore his new territory, and give him a name, preferably one with two syllables. If he cries in the night, give him a hot-water bottle. Don't chastise him unduly; after all, he's just a little man. Take him for a walk. Talk to him. Look after him. He will reward you with many happy years of loyal companionship.

THE CAT CAME BACK

The whole thing began because of overpopulation, war and a global ecological disaster. Which led to a complete breakdown of law and order and an outbreak of violent crime on a massive scale. Which led to universal demoralisation and a catastrophic worldwide economic depression. Which meant that he lost his job and began squabbling with his wife. Which caused him, one morning, to go out and kick the dog, which bit the cat and ate its food. Causing the cat to leave home in a huff and hide under the neighbour's house for three days.

Three days! For three days they fretted and pined and nobody slept a wink. Until the cat came back. Blessed relief! The cat came back.

SYDNEY

Sydney seems to invite judgement. It provokes sweeping statements, gross generalisations and complicated oversimplifications about its very nature. I am going there hoping to see or hear something which will represent to me the essence of Sydney.

Travelling there on a plane, I talk with a person who says to me the following words: 'Sydney! It's all fairy lights and cockroaches and hot chips and burglar alarms.' Upon arrival, I make my way to a favourite spot – the kiosk at the end of the Opera House, where it juts into the harbour – hoping for a simple sandwich and a cup of tea. But alas, the people's kiosk has gone and I find instead a glassed-in expensive restaurant. Is this it, so early in my mission? Is this scene the essence of Sydney?

I wander through the swarming tourists to the botanical gardens, where I inspect the site of Australia's first farm. A sign tells me that the venture was a failure. Can this be a clue to the nature of Sydney? Could it be that all simple, goodly and honest attempts at productivity are destined to fail here? A place fit only for slick entrepreneurs?

Onward to the art gallery, and there I see the Archibald Prize entries, including a portrait of an old friend, Patrick Cook. He is at least double life-sized. He seems huge and healthy and golden. He seems more real than the Patrick I know. Is there some lesson in this? Is this what happens in Sydney?

Burdened with omens, I struggle to Kings Cross, where I see many people drugged and stoned and wretched, like tranquillised stray dogs waiting to be put down in a dirty, smelly veterinary clinic. I walk across town. All about are traffic and fumes and noise and steamy odours. Beggars beg, drunks rant and scream. In Glebe I see graffiti which says 'Lentil Nightmare'.

I buy a half-bottle of wine. The woman serving me hardly takes her eyes off a blaring television set standing by the cash register. This strikes me as a profoundly significant scene. A lonely dinner, and I decide to call on a friend. The lights are on but nobody is at home. I check the back of the house and there I smell frangipani and hear a frog croaking. This used to be part of the essence of Sydney.

Soon after this, I see a restaurant called Vince Thai and Spanish Vietnamese Restaurant, and it is at this point that I decide to go back to my hotel near Circular Quay and begin reading a novel called *Dead Souls* by the Russian writer Nikolai Gogol.

I wake to Australia Day. The quay is alive with flag-sellers, buskers, drunks and tourists. One old busker makes music on a saw. This is significant. In Melbourne, a saw is used for cutting wood. In Sydney, a saw is used for making music.

I take the Manly ferry. From the rear deck I watch the

Harbour Bridge and the Opera House receding across the water in the morning sunshine. It is as beautiful and dignified a sight as it ever was. Life is heart-wrenching and joyous. How unlucky are Sydneysiders that they run the risk of growing used to this sight. How lucky are the others, who can visit this place and travel through it somewhat innocently.

Ferry travellers wave to people in small boats. The people in small boats wave back. For fleeting moments across the dark water, there is simple cheerfulness and goodwill. This is a miracle! Seated on the deck, a young couple cuddle dreamily. The air is balmy. The swell rolls the ferry softly and pleasantly, and so gives assistance to their cuddling, and tenderly, with all the irresistible, heaving power of nature, confirms their kisses. Perhaps *this* is the essence of Sydney?

I turn away from the lovers and stare down into the water. A half-submerged Akubra hat drifts by. I return to the Opera House for the official Australia Day ceremony, and there I see and hear the Premier, the Archbishop, the Lord Mayor, the Governor . . . all the most dubious types of people. An old lady in the crowd yells out, 'Bullshit!' and is reprimanded by the police. Perhaps this is the essence of Sydney? Is Sydney a place where people are punished for being truthful? I wonder.

A homeless old man in a wheelchair lives under the railway viaduct at Circular Quay. He is ill and undernourished. Does he reveal more about the state of Sydney than Ken Done? And whose Akubra hat was that I saw floating in the harbour?

I ride the monorail. I go to the Darling Harbour complex. I see buskers, avant-garde performance artists by the score, criminals in luxury powerboats, vast surging oceans of tourists, beer cans, wine bottles, junk food, glass, steel and concrete. Why have they turned this city into a giant fun park? Why does the solitary traveller here feel so lonely, so tired, so ripped off? If they're so clever, why didn't they make it more *humane*? Why does everything have to be so BIG and so crowded? Why are the police batons so long? Why does a cup of tea cost so much? How come there's nothing to do but to look and to buy?

'Heavenly father, help us to resist the overtures of greed and selfishness,' said the Archbishop in his Australia Day prayer. 'Sydney, the best address on earth,' said the Lord Mayor. Why do so many people wear the T-shirt saying, 'Don't Worry, Be Happy'? Why do people drink so much alcohol? Why do tourists take so many photographs? Whose hat was that in the harbour?

I go back to my hotel. Outside, the night sky is full of fireworks and police sirens. I go to bed and read *Dead Souls*.

THE CLIMB

LONDON, Wed. — An American stuntman hoping
to become the first person to swim the English
Channel with his hands and feet bound gave up
after only 6.4 km today.

I was inspired. I decided to be the first human to climb Mount
Everest bound and gagged. I made it to the front gate of my
Footscray home with no problems. Then I fell down and rolled
into the gutter. It started to rain, but I was undaunted – I had
Mount Everest on the brain. The gutter was awash and litter
piled up around me. Then it happened – the surging torrent
pushed me forward. I was on my way!

After several hours, I arrived at a drain about ten yards down
the street. My head entered it; I decided to establish a base camp.
I fell asleep and dreamed wild, joyous dreams about Everest,
which now lay within my grasp.

'Great deeds and great thoughts all have a ridiculous
beginning.'
                                                    – Albert Camus

GUNK I

He woke up completely covered in gunk. All around him, everything in the room was covered in gunk. And outside, too, the streets, the houses, the entire city seemed to be covered in gunk. People everywhere were smothered in it; gunk had worked its way into and onto everything and everyone.

How tired, heavy and dull it made the world! Nothing sparkled any more, nothing moved freely. What *was* it? What was this gunk? What was it composed of, where did it come from, and what was to be done about it? Why were so many people *promoting* it?

GUNK II

Covered in gunk, he visited a wise elder to discuss this mysterious substance which covered not only his body, but the entire world. 'I feel like my whole life – my feelings, my actions – are covered with an invisible, numbing, clammy sludge. How can this be? What *is* this gunk?'

'Gunk is the material which holds the modern world together. Certainly it is an encumbrance, but without it our lives and our civilisations would probably fall apart. Gunk is the glue of existence.'

'There's an awful lot of it about. It seems to get worse every day. Has the world always been covered in gunk?'

'Good heavens, no! The world used to be held together with *inner* structures, and, as you can tell, gunk is an external matter. It holds things together from the outside. It's like a packing material which stops everything cracking and breaking. It's a sort of shredded waste which surrounds everything and everybody and keeps things from actually touching.'

'The trouble is, it's very stifling. Very gooey.'

'Yes, I feel like I'm stewing in my own juice all the time – and in everybody else's as well.'

'Well, what's it made of, this packaging material? This coating, this gunk?'

'Forgive me if this seems a bit crude, but gunk is a mish-mash blend of a million and one varieties of one hundred percent bullshit, and we're all absolutely covered in it!'

How to Dig a Nice Hole
to Rest Your Soul In

Take a spade and find a quiet place where the ground is not too hard. Dig a nice hole. Not too big, not too small. One that feels good, secure and well rounded. Admire what you have done. Get down and smell the perfume of the soil. Observe any worms or small creatures in the earth.

Now place your weary soul carefully and comfortably in the beautiful hole. Whisper to your soul, 'There, there, everything's going to be all right. You just rest for as long as you like.' Then perhaps you might take a rest yourself, or go for a gentle walk, but don't worry, your soul will be safe and peaceful and very, very happy.

DEATHBED

I am on my deathbed, cold and alone in a dim, sordid room. Through the window I see the city in a greyish, yellow smoke haze. A rocket streaks across the evening sky. Everything is lost. Suddenly some type of angel is present and tells me I can be granted a few minutes of my past to live over again. I am asked to choose which few minutes I want.

Without thinking, I say I would dearly love any few minutes; anything at all would be precious. And suddenly I am standing in a paddock of dry grass in the country. The sky is deep blue. The sun glitters through the leaves of a large red gum. It is late afternoon. There are two children, a pond. Magpies sing. How precious! I am standing in a simple and wonderful vision, ecstatic, tranquil. If only I had loved my entire life as I loved these few minutes' reprieve from death!

Just then the sun flashes in my eyes and it dawns on me. This is no reprieve, this *is* my life. These trees, these magpies, this sunlight, this rusty old bed in the pond.

Amazing Facts About the Twentieth Century

If all the cars manufactured during the twentieth century were melted down and made into one big car, the front bumper bar would be found at the West Footscray post office, and the rear bumper would be located at the Box Hill shopping plaza. If the car was parked near Albury, the radio aerial would be a hazard to jets flying between Sydney and Melbourne. The ashtray in the dashboard would be four times as big as the Melbourne Cricket Ground; the fuel tank would hold the entire contents of Westernport Bay at high tide.

If the car got a flat tyre, it would take the Premier of Victoria one entire week to talk it up again. If the car skidded out of control, overturned and burst into flames, the Prime Minister would come stumbling out of the wreckage and say, 'What's the problem? I always park the car like that!'

THE GATE

In the corner of his lounge room stood a wooden box with a glass panel at the front and a vase of flowers on top. This box was flippantly known as a television and was supposed to be a window on the world. In reality it was more like a tap, a valve or a gate, and when the man pressed a button the gate opened. And into his room, into his eyes, his brain and his spirit, rushed a powerful and complicated substance.

Every night he would open this gate and sit in front of it, exposing himself to an enormous flow of the powerful substance, completely unprotected. Every world crisis; every horror; everything hideous, ugly, artificial, insincere, freakish, violent, stupid, crass, loud and phoney from the entire world was blended, concentrated and funnelled through the gate into his once humble Home, Sweet Home. Through his eyes, into his frail dreams, and onto the tiny painted memories of innocence which hung lopsided in his heart. Completely unprotected!

THE MISSING UNDERPANTS

He awoke to find that his underpants were missing. He went searching and met the milkman, who told him that he had seen a pair of underpants moving like a ghost along the foggy street in the direction of the paddock. He ran to the paddock and there in a ditch he found the tattered remains of his underpants.

On his way home he met an old man who said that on the previous night he had shot a pair of underpants which had been devouring his chickens for the past two weeks. At least that explained the feathers inside his underpants on recent mornings, but it didn't explain why his life was degenerating into an uncontrollable farce.

How to Pay
Your Way and Stand
on Your Own Feet

God's grace, nature's blessings, free music from the birds – these mollycoddling handouts make us soft and uncompetitive. It's time to get real and become a self-made winner!

First you must create your own air and water, so you will need a large, reliable chemistry set and some strong storage vessels. Then you must provide your own sunlight and soil, and for this you will require huge quantities of various inflammable gases and a box of matches, plus a secure lava supply and machinery for crushing and grinding. Then it's just a matter of putting in the hours and the hard work and watching the whole thing multiply. And until you have done all this, until you have spurned all those subsidies from heaven – the moonlight, the flowers, the sunrise, etc., which weaken us so – and until you have made it entirely on your own, you are not real.

THE FALLEN ANGEL

It was the night before Christmas and the angel, who should have been singing in the heavens, was too weary to fly and too depressed to sing. Sadly and aimlessly he wandered the city streets, feeling lonelier and lonelier as his wings grew dirtier and more tattered on the pavement. He passed a mirror in a shop and was shocked to see how haggard and deranged he looked – how corrupted and miserable.

'For a small sum I can ease your pain,' said a voice from a doorway, and soon a syringe had entered his wing and he lay down in an alley and slept. And as the traffic roared about him, the angel dreamed of his childhood and of something even more distant and more beautiful and mysterious. Until at last, still sleeping, he rose free from the city of pain and returned to where he truly belonged – to the manger and the animals and to all his friends, singing their hearts out.

Time to Get Your Tomatoes In

Tending your tomato plants is one of life's great simple pleasures, but there are pitfalls. Tomato stakes are best hammered in under the cover of darkness, to avoid being spotted by trade-union officials. Bikie wars and shootouts in the garden during flowering can seriously affect cropping. Nuclear winter, caused by global nuclear war, can delay ripening.

On the brighter side, the chances of catching genital herpes or AIDS from handling tomatoes are fairly low. Certainly, tomato tending has its worries, but it's all worthwhile when you stand in the garden on a warm summer's day and sink your fangs into a firm, ripe, freshly picked tomato.

Venerable, Blessed and Saintly Creatures

Bess the Dog

Saint Bess of the Compassionate Gaze. Canonised for her work among the urban depressed and for the miracles associated with her healing eyes. Saint Bess was never known to speak in her entire life.

Roger the Cat

The venerable Roger of the Cobblestones. For one half of his life, Roger of the Cobblestones lived a life of utter depravity. For the other half, he devoted himself to prayer and contemplation. Prayer and contemplation by day, utter depravity by night.

Waldo the Canary

The most Blessed Waldo the Innocent of Yarraville. Waldo the gasworks canary was beatified for his devotion to liturgical and sacred music, in spite of being cruelly incarcerated for life.

Marjorie the Milking Cow

Saint Marjorie of Gippsland. She lived on prickles and weeds, yet achieved serenity and managed to nourish the weary multitudes with her miraculous abundance of cream and milk. Marjorie was martyred late in life as a result of a deal between her owner and a pet-food manufacturer.

THE APACHE

The noble Apache people were brutally crushed by the American invaders, who took away their land and named a helicopter after them. The Apache helicopter is now used to invade other countries, to crush people and take their land. But all in the name of democracy, of course, and all under the name of freedom, and all with the name of the noble, insurgent Apache.

THE GARDEN

You go into the garden. It's a good place to grow. You pull out a little weed, and some nasty little worry leaves your mind. How fascinating! And there! A tiny ant. So bright and brave. It could be you. Could it?

And look at that rose! You are reminded of your true love. So beautiful, and with sharp thorns.

Now contemplate the compost heap. It's just like your mind, your memory, your history. Breaking down but getting richer.

Aha! The trellis. Full of beans and peas. You need a trellis sometimes. We all need a little support.

Oh dear. A stem has broken. Something has come to nothing. A hope is dashed. But it's okay, you will grow back. The sun will shine again.

But look at that beautiful, luxuriant fern! You are reminded of the book you want to write. Some sort of fabulous unfurling from some exotic part of your mind.

A bird sings and flits by. It scratches in the soil. Your heart is a bird. It flies up towards the sun. The creeper needs cutting back. The petty worries, the nagging inhibitions, the nasty and the narrow. Those who drag you down. Cut yourself free!

Oh, look at that! A new leaf! You can always turn over a new leaf. It will turn itself back again of course.

Ah yes, the garden. The fruits, the shoots, the blooms. The fragrance. The light and the shade. And you – you are in love and growing.

THE CONTEST

And now, the great contest we've been waiting for between the truth and the prime minister. They're in their starting positions. The crowd is hushed, waiting for the signal. They're away!

The truth confronts the prime minister, but the prime minister steps aside and twists the truth in an amazing manoeuvre. The prime minister is twisting the truth, twisting. Twisting . . . twisting . . . and it's all over! What a sensation! The truth is beaten! The prime minister has made it look so easy. What a champion! That's gold for Australia! Pure, simple gold!

Interview with God

God, who are your chosen people?
This week, Sheryl and Bert Boggleton are my chosen people.
Really? How come? Who are they?
Well, they're just a good old couple, and I like them.
Okay, sure.
They're not perfect or anything; they have their ups and downs of course.
What privileges will now flow to them?
Nothing, really. They don't seem to need special privileges, that's what I like about them. They're genuine, humble people, and kind of sweet. I like 'em.

LAYER UPON LAYER

An entire civilisation buried under layer upon layer of lies, untruths and falsehoods! A civilisation suffocated and frozen in time; trapped beneath a huge deluge of spin! People's last dramatic moments preserved forever by an almighty shower of Weasel words. Humans unable to flee. A civilisation entombed. A whole culture tangled in twaddle, mummified in ridiculous poses of bewilderment . . .

WHY IS IT CALLED
BOXING DAY?

The box was invented on 26 December 1602 in Ely, Cambridgeshire, England and is named after its inventor, George Rupert Box, who was trying to create a new type of drinking vessel using five pieces of flat wood. His invention was ahead of its time, for nobody could think of a use for it until a neighbour, Daniel Robert Lid, created the final touch for the device on 1 June 1609.

The 'lid', as it became known in honour of its inventor, saved the box from extinction, and the 'box with lid' spread rapidly and changed the world. It is indeed strange that while we still celebrate Boxing Day on 26 December, Lidding Day on 1 June seems to have been forgotten, lost in the mists of time. How very, very odd!